W9-COO-769

Contemporary African Americans

BEN CARSON

BY
ALEX SIMMONS

RSVP
RAINTREE
STECK-VAUGHN
PUBLISHERS
The Steck-Vaughn Company

Austin, Texas

Published by Raintree Steck-Vaughn, an imprint of Steck-Vaughn Company.
Produced by Mega-Books, Inc.
Design and Art Direction by Michaelis/Carpelis Design Associates.
Cover photo: Courtesy Johns Hopkins Medical Institutions.

Library of Congress Cataloging-in-Publication Data
Simmons, Alex.
      Ben Carson / by Alex Simmons.
         p. cm.— (Contemporaty African Americans)
      Includes bibliographical references and index.
      Summary: A biography of the surgeon who overcame poverty and racism to become chief of pediatric neurosurgery at Johns Hopkins University Hospital.
      ISBN 0-8172-3975-8 (Hardcover)
      ISBN 0-8114-9793-3 (Softcover)
      1. Carson, Ben—Juvenile literature. 2. Neurosurgeons—United States—Biography—Juvenile literature. 3. Afro-American surgeons—United States—Biography—Juvenile literature. [1. Carson, Ben. 2. Neurosurgeons. 3. Physicians 4. Afro-Americans—Biography.]
      I. Title II. Series.
RD592.9.C37S56   1996
617.4'8'092—dc20   95-12732
[B]   CIP
                                   AC

Printed and bound in the United States.

1 2 3 4 5 6 7 8 9 LB 99 98 97 96 95

Photo credits: Courtesy Johns Hopkins Medical Institutions: pp. 6, 9, 13, 20, 23, 24, 26, 29, 31, 32, 35, 39, 41, 42; The Bettmann Archive: p.7; Peter Serling: pp. 10, 36, 44; AP/Wide WorldPhotos: p. 15; UPI/Bettmann Newsphotos: p. 18; William De Kay/*Detroit Free Press*: p. 16.

Contents

Chapter One

IN THE OR

The clock in the hospital operating room (OR) ticks away the seconds between life and death. As the hands of the clock move slowly around, Dr. Benjamin Carson uses a **scalpel** to cut through a child's tender skin. Then, Dr. Carson cuts away a section of the child's skull. Slowly removing the piece of bone, he stares down at the brain of four-year-old Maranda Francisco.

In this brain is the cause of years of pain for Maranda. If Dr. Carson can find the problem and remove it, he can save the girl from her pain. Then Maranda will finally have a normal life. But one wrong move could end in permanent damage to Maranda. One slip of the doctor's hand could even mean the girl's death.

The amazing surgical skills of Dr. Ben Carson have relieved the suffering of dozens of children. Here, Dr. Carson spends time with a three-year-old patient.

In the operating room, minutes grow into hours. Two hours go by, then five… then ten….

Imagine doing something that takes every bit of your attention for ten hours straight—or even twenty! Then, imagine a little girl's life depends on your doing that task just right. Her parents have placed their child's life in your hands. They are pacing nervously in the hospital waiting room.

Dr. Ben Carson has worked under this kind of pressure for a long time. In recent years, every time he steps into the operating room, his patient is a child.

Dr. Carson is the Chief of Pediatric Neurosurgery at Johns Hopkins Hospital, in Baltimore, Maryland. **Pediatrics** is the area of medicine that focuses on children. **Neurosurgery** deals with operations on a person's brain or other parts of their nervous system. Dr. Ben Carson specializes in operating on the brains of children.

Ben Carson is the first African American to hold this position at Johns Hopkins. This is quite an achievement. He has also performed major operations that have changed medical history. For these reasons, Dr. Carson stands among the many other African Americans who have made medical history. For example, in 1867, Dr. Rebecca Cole became one of the first African-American women doctors in the United States. In 1893, Dr. Daniel Hale Williams, also African American, performed the world's first successful open-heart surgery.

African-American pioneers in medicine, such as surgeon Daniel Hale Williams, helped to pave the way for gifted black doctors like Ben Carson.

To join these ranks, Ben Carson overcame nearly impossible odds. Many lucky children know that Ben saved their lives. What they do not know is that he went from living in poor neighborhoods in Detroit and Boston to working in one of the best hospitals in the country. His journey makes quite a story. It is a story of anger, racism, pride, faith, determination—and the power of love.

Chapter Two

HIDING THE HURT

"Your daddy isn't coming back." These were the words Mrs. Sonya Carson spoke to her ten-year-old son, Curtis, and her eight-year-old son, Benjamin, in 1959. Their father had left, and their parents were getting a divorce.

Sonya Carson knew things were going to be rough. She had no way of earning money. Her small house in Detroit, Michigan, was more than she could afford to keep. And worries over money were not the only things that hurt. Mrs. Carson and her two children ached with the pain of broken hearts.

For young Ben Carson, the problem boiled down to a very simple fact: Daddy was gone. Ben recalls the pain and the confusion he felt after his father left. Mr. Carson had always been loving and devoted to his sons. He had never given the boys any reason to think that one day he would leave forever. Ben begged his mother to set things right, and he prayed that his

Dr. Ben Carson experienced painful and difficult times when he was a child. Today, his gentle and caring ways help bring his young patients through their own painful times.

father would come home. It was no use. He was gone for good. Soon, Ben learned to hide the deep pain of losing his father.

Ben's mother, too, tried to ignore her feelings. Instead she focused on taking care of her family. Mrs. Carson was determined to make a good life for her two sons. To earn money, she took many jobs. Mostly, she cleaned and cooked in other people's homes. Sonya Carson's life had never been very easy. She had only gone to school through the third grade. For a woman who could barely read or write, good jobs were not easy to find. Still, she worked hard, and she never complained.

As the months passed, things got even harder for

Mrs. Carson. With her husband gone, Ben's mother struggled just to keep food on the table and a roof over their heads. Bills piled up. Ben and his brother Curtis often asked for candy or toys that their mother could not afford to buy. Ben began to see how worried and hurt his mother looked whenever she did not have the money to get by.

When all the difficulties became too much for her, Sonya Carson made a difficult decision. "I'm going to visit some relatives," she told her sons. She explained that she needed to go alone. The boys would stay with some of her friends.

Dr. Ben Carson gives much of the credit for his success to his mother, Sonya Carson. She was always a strong and loving parent, even when times were hardest.

In truth, Mrs. Carson's "visits" were actually stays at a psychiatric hospital. Sonya's mental health was suffering. Whenever she felt too much pressure, Sonya checked herself into a hospital for help. She did not tell Ben where she had really gone until he was an adult. Mrs. Carson thought it was best to keep her troubles hidden from Ben and his brother. It was one of her ways of trying to protect the boys.

Even with Mrs. Carson's stays at the hospital, things continued to get worse. Ben's mother could not keep up with the house payments. By the fall of 1959, Ben and his family had to move out of their home in Detroit. His mother rented out the house. She took the boys to live with her older sister, Jean, and Jean's husband, William Avery. The Averys lived in Boston, Massachusetts.

Ben's father drove the family to their new home. It was one of the few times Ben would see his father after the divorce. It had been a difficult year for the young boy. He had already lost part of his family. Now, he was losing his home. For Ben, there were hard times still to come—but there were also new dreams to experience.

Three

CHANGES AND CHALLENGES

Christmas, 1959, was the best Christmas Ben had ever had. His aunt, uncle, and mother showered the two Carson boys with love and with presents. Ben's favorite present was a chemistry set. He spent hours and hours doing science experiments. He tested chemicals on special paper. He created foul-smelling mixtures in the sink. It was exciting!

To Ben, the chemistry set meant much more than just playtime. It was like a gateway to a dream. Ben's dream for the future had begun one Sunday at church, back in Detroit. The Carsons were Seventh-Day Adventists. At one church service, their pastor told a very exciting story about a missionary doctor and his wife, who were being chased by deadly bandits in a faraway country. They had survived, the pastor said, with the help of the Lord.

Listening to the story, Ben's head was filled with thoughts of travel, danger, and helping people in a

Curtis (left) and Ben Carson faced many changes as they grew up, but Christmas was always a special time in the Carson family.

distant land. The pastor's story excited Ben so much he decided that he, too, wanted to become a missionary doctor. He had no idea how it would all happen, but he felt he had found his place in life. Ben told his mother about his plan. She told him he could be whatever he wanted to be. As far as Mrs. Carson was concerned, nothing could stop her boys. With her love and care, Ben and Curtis would grow strong and whole.

Ben's mother was not the only one supporting him. His Aunt Jean and Uncle William had a lot of love to share. The Averys' own children were already grown up and living away from home. Jean and William Avery treated Ben and Curtis as two of their own. When Mrs. Carson needed to go to the hospital, the Averys were always ready to care for the boys.

Even though the Averys made the Carsons feel at home, Ben still felt uncomfortable. Life in Boston was unlike life in Detroit. Back home, the Carsons had lived in a house. The house was plain and simple, but the neighborhood was always well kept. Here, things were different. The Averys' apartment was in one of the poorest neighborhoods in Boston. Rats roamed the alleyways, and there was also litter and broken glass everywhere. Police sirens wailed in the background. Painfully, Ben and Curtis realized they had to adjust to Boston. Like it or not, this was now home.

The Carson boys began attending school. Ben did not see much of his mother. She often had to work two or three jobs each day. She would come home from work very tired. Still, Sonya Carson would check in with her boys about their schoolwork. Ben knew that education was very important to his mother.

After a while, Ben saw that life was really better without his father. He remembered that his parents had not talked to each other much. Often the silence in their home had frightened him. Now, at the Averys' home, he and Curtis felt more at peace.

In 1961, after two years of working hard and saving money, Sonya Carson was able to move the family back to Detroit. At first, they lived in an apartment in the city's industrial area. Nearby were car factories and railroad tracks.

School in Detroit was a terrible shock to Ben. In Boston, his grades had been good. But when he entered Higgins Elementary School in Detroit, the other fifth graders were way ahead of him in math, English, history—everything! Many students poked fun at him. If there was a wrong answer to a question, they were sure that Ben Carson would give it.

Ben Carson spent most of his childhood in inner-city Detroit. Many neighborhoods were segregated, and some African-American communities faced poverty and hopelessness.

Unlike his school in Boston, Higgins had mostly white students. Nobody ever said anything mean about Ben being black. Still, the more he failed in class, the more Ben began to believe that maybe black children were not as smart as white children. He feared other students felt the same way.

Ben never said a word about this fear to his mother or his teachers. Again, he kept his pain hidden deep inside. Mrs. Carson always gave both her sons words of support and inspiration. "I've got two smart boys," she often told Ben and Curtis. Ben admits he and his brother did not always want to listen to their mother, but she would not give up. She believed that bright futures were awaiting her sons.

Ben remembers his mother's faith and her strong will to help her sons. "Though we might have to read more and study longer," Ben recalls, "my mother was determined that Curtis and I would succeed." Ben's mother formed a plan to make sure this happened. She began going over every homework assignment with the boys. She insisted that Ben memorize his

Sonya Carson's faith and guidance would help both her sons succeed in life.

multiplication tables. Though he did not like it much, Ben did as he was told. He never thought about going against his mother's wishes.

Mrs. Carson also cut back on how much time the boys could watch television. When they were not doing their homework, Mrs. Carson insisted they read instead of watching TV. In fact, Ben and Curtis had to read two books each week. They even had to turn in a book report to their mother when they were finished.

Slowly the boys' grades began to improve. Ben's interest in his studies grew as he began to understand more. He also learned that books could take him anywhere he wanted to go. It did not matter how much money he had or where he lived. Books gave him adventure. Books gave him knowledge. By his last year at Higgins, Ben was one of the top students in his class. Many of the very children who had once teased him now came to him for help.

After Ben left Higgins, however, racial prejudice entered his life. It was now the 1960s, and African Americans had begun to fight for equal rights. Some white people were resisting change, and real tensions were building.

Ben joined his brother Curtis at Wilson Junior High School. People began to notice Ben's intelligence and hard work. Every year, Wilson gave an award to its most outstanding student. Ben received the award two years in a row. At the second award ceremony, one of Ben's teachers handed Ben his award, then turned and

Nonviolent protests like this one were an important part of the African American struggle for equal rights in the 1960s. Ben Carson, like many black people, faced racism from whites who were resisting change.

spoke to the audience. What she said came as a surprise. She put down the white students for allowing Ben to beat them! Ben remembers that her speech was not openly racist, but her meaning was clear: A black person should never be number one in anything. At first, Ben felt angry and confused. Then, he decided this teacher did not know what she was saying.

This was not the first time Ben had faced racism. A gang of white boys had stopped him on his way to school. They threatened him with a big stick, and told him, "You niggers ain't supposed to be going to Wilson... If we ever catch you again, we're going to kill you." After that, Ben had to find another route to get to school. Later, when Ben and Curtis Carson joined a neighborhood football league, a group of young white men cornered them. They told the Carson boys they would be thrown into the river if they returned to practice. Neither Ben nor his brother ever told Mrs. Carson about these racist threats. They did not want their mother to worry about them.

So far, silence had been Ben's way to survive. He did not talk about his father leaving him. He did not talk about kids teasing him when he did poorly in school. The racist acts of white people, the threats—all this Ben Carson kept to himself. But where were all his hurt and anger going? They did not just disappear into thin air. Toward the end of the eighth grade, all Ben's hurt began to boil over.

Mrs. Carson announced to her sons that she had enough money for the family to move back to their old house. Ben and Curtis were happy to be going home. However, the move meant that Ben had to transfer to the junior high in his old neighborhood. Unlike Wilson, Hunter Junior High School had mostly black students. Here, race was not a problem. What mattered was how you acted and what clothes you wore. Ben did not always fit in. He became the target of kids who liked to put others down.

Ben tried to ignore those kids. He told himself that what they said did not matter—but it did. Ben began to let his intelligence and quick wit work for him. He

Young Ben Carson would overcome anger and frustration to take control of his life.

started talking back. The other students slowly began to accept him. Soon, playing basketball and hanging out after school became more important to Ben than his studies. His mother tried to keep him focused on school work, but Ben began to rebel.

In high school, clothes also became very important to Ben. He knew his mother could not afford to buy him the latest fashions, yet Ben kept asking for the impossible. Once, Mrs. Carson bought him a pair of pants that were not stylish enough. When his mother insisted he wear them, Ben flew into a rage. He moved to hit her. His brother Curtis leaped on Ben and held him back until Ben could get control of himself.

This was not the first time Ben's anger had become dangerous. Back at Wilson, a classmate had once teased Ben about a wrong answer Ben gave in English class. Ben had struck the boy in the head with a padlock. The blow had caused bleeding. Ben later had apologized from his heart. Another time, a neighborhood boy threw a small stone at Ben. In a flash, Ben found a large rock and threw it with all his might. He broke the child's nose. Ben's temper was out of control, but he did not see how big the problem was. His friends, his brother, and even his mother were not safe from Ben's rage.

The final burst of anger came in 1965, when Ben was in ninth grade. One day, he and his friend, Bob, were listening to the radio. Bob made fun of Ben's taste in music and began to change the station. Without a second thought, Ben grabbed a camping knife. He flicked it open and lunged at Bob's belly. This one act of violence would change Ben Carson's life forever.

Four

CUTS BOTH WAYS

Ben stood frozen, staring down at the knife blade. It lay broken on the sidewalk. Luckily, Bob was wearing a metal belt buckle. The force of Ben's thrust had been incredible, but an inch of metal had saved Bob's life.

In a way, it saved Ben's life, too. Filled with fear and horror at his own actions, Ben ran home and locked himself in the bathroom. For several hours he wept and cursed. He had almost murdered his friend! Was this what his life had become? Was he really ruled by acts of rage and violence? And what about his dream to become a doctor? Was he headed for prison rather than medical school? He could find no answers.

Now came a turning point in his life. Kneeling there on the cold tile floor, 14-year-old Ben Carson prayed as he had never prayed before. He pleaded for help in winning out over his temper. Ben remembers something very important happened. He felt the weight of his troubles lift from his shoulders. He felt something dangerous leave his soul. Ben says that when he walked out of that bathroom, he was whole, peaceful, and calm. He never lost control again.

Faith had always been the answer in Ben's life. His mother had faith that she could hold the family together and raise her boys right. Ben had faith in the love and strength of his family, and even in himself. Now, Ben also had faith that God was going to see him through life as he worked his way toward becoming a doctor. From then on, Ben kept his temper under control and picked up his books.

When he entered high school, Curtis Carson had become a member of the Reserve Officers' Training Corps (ROTC) program. Ben decided to do the same.

The Reserve Officers' Training Corps (ROTC) helped Ben Carson (third from left) discover and develop his leadership skills.

During ROTC training, Ben discovered he was a strong leader. His good grades were noticed and encouraged by his ROTC leaders. By the time Ben graduated from high school, he was a colonel in the ROTC. In two and a half years, he had climbed to a rank that normally took three or four years to reach.

In 1969, young Colonel Ben Carson marched at the head of the Detroit Memorial Day Parade. He had dinner with General William Westmoreland and two other honored soldiers of the Vietnam War. Ben was

By the time he graduated high school in 1969, Ben Carson was back on the way to achieving his dreams. Here Ben (left) poses beside his brother Curtis and Carson family friends.

also offered a full scholarship to West Point Military Academy. He thought the offer over, but in the end he turned it down. His desire to go to medical school was even stronger.

During his last year of high school, Ben had to choose a college. Because of his grades and his great record in the ROTC, many colleges and universities wanted him. However, each college application cost ten dollars. Ben had only a single ten-dollar bill, which meant he could only apply to one school. Ben could not decide which college to choose.

Ben made his choice one night when he was watching an episode of his favorite TV quiz show, *College Bowl*. Teams on the show were from colleges around the country. Each team had to answer difficult questions in order to earn points. The questions covered everything from military history to classical music. Ben himself had learned a lot about classical music in case he ever went on the show.

In this episode, students from Yale University beat the Harvard University team, 510 to 35. That was an amazing score! Ben knew instantly that Yale was the school for him. He applied and was accepted in a matter of weeks. Yale also offered Ben an academic scholarship that would cover almost all of his costs. With that news, Ben was soon on his way to New Haven, Connecticut, to begin his studies at Yale.

Ben felt pretty good about himself when he entered Yale in the fall of 1969. After all, he had

At Yale, Ben's hard work and dedication helped him succeed in the premed program.

graduated third in his class in high school. He had also been accepted by one of the best universities in the country. Ben thought he could not go wrong.

Within a week, however, Ben saw that he was not as well-prepared as many of his classmates. Once again, he felt like the dumb one in a room filled with geniuses. Ben worked hard, but by the end of his first semester, he was failing chemistry. Without that class, he could not stay in the premedical program. Premed was the program he needed to follow so he could later go to medical school. He had to do better!

The day before the chemistry exam, Ben wandered around the campus. He had studied hard for the exam, but he still felt worried and hopeless. All his negative thoughts began to take over. Who was he trying to fool? He was a black kid from a poor neighborhood. He could not make it at Yale.

Ben went back to his room and studied one more time for the exam. By midnight, he had memorized all he could. He was tired. His head and eyes hurt from so much reading. Once again, Ben turned to his faith. Becoming a doctor was all he had ever wanted. He prayed for guidance and help.

According to Ben, he had a special dream that night. In the dream, he was sitting in his classroom, waiting to take his exam. A shadowy figure walked in and began writing the questions on the chalkboard. Ben started to work out the problems. He discovered each correct answer as he went along.

When Ben woke up, most of the dream was still fresh in his mind. He ran to the chemistry room to take the exam. His whole future depended on this test. Ben's palms were sweating as he opened the test booklet. He was shocked when he skimmed over the questions. They were just like the ones in his dream! He knew the answers. He went right to work on the exam problems. When the grades were finally posted, he got a very high score of 97. Now he was at the top of his class!

For the next four years, Ben felt certain that he was going to become a doctor. He kept up his grades. He studied harder. He read even more than his teachers assigned.

His studies were not the only things that were

improving in Ben's life. At the beginning of his third year at Yale, Ben met a new student, Lacena Candy Rustin.They became good friends. Candy shared Ben's love of books and music. She played the violin with the Yale Symphony. She even joined the choir at Ben's church near the university.

Late one night, Ben and Candy were near the end of a long drive. Candy dozed off in the passenger's seat. A little while later, Ben nodded off at the wheel. Just as the car was heading for a deep ravine, Ben snapped awake. When he yanked on the steering wheel, the car spun wildly. Ben was certain they were going to die. Instead, the car settled back on the highway. A second later, a tractor-trailer truck roared by. If it had passed a moment sooner, the truck would have crushed Ben and Candy's car.

Candy woke up. She did not know what had just happened. After Ben explained they had nearly been killed, they both decided that they must be alive for a reason. From that time on, Ben and Candy were always together.

Ben spent his summers working at different jobs. He supervised a road crew, delivered packages, and worked on an auto assembly line. Each job made Ben feel good about working hard and earning money.

In 1973, Ben Carson graduated from Yale. He had completed the four-year premed program. Ben was accepted by the medical school at the University of Michigan. Because he was from Michigan, school costs

Ben celebrates his graduation from Yale University. With him are Sonya Carson and Candy Rustin.

would be much lower there. It was also an excellent medical school.

Medical school was much harder than Yale had ever been. Still, it was here that Ben discovered his true skills. Again, Ben Carson would put a knife in his hand. But this time it was to save lives, not take them.

DOING THE
IMPOSSIBLE

During his first two years at the University of Michigan, Ben read each textbook from cover to cover. He studied from six o'clock in the morning until eleven o'clock at night. His goal was to have a full understanding of every subject. He was working hard to become the best doctor he could be.

Ben's third year in medical school was his clinical year. This is the time when medical students work in hospitals. They work for a month in each area of hospital medicine. One month Ben was introduced to neurosurgery. That month would change his life.

While watching a brain operation, Ben saw that the surgeon was having a hard time finding a special spot in the skull. Ben figured out a better way to do this. Shyly, he showed his professors the new method. They were amazed! Ben was pleased with his discovery. He was happy about something else, as well. He had discovered he loved neurosurgery. In fact, he liked it

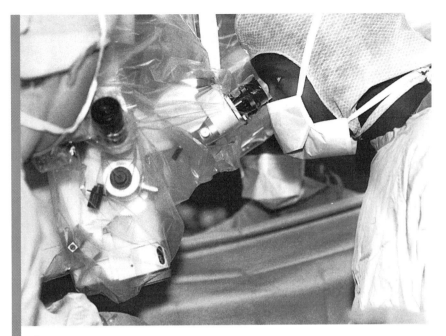

During his hospital training, Ben Carson discovered his love of neurosurgery. This, along with his natural ability, would soon take him to the top of his field.

so much that he was allowed to spend an extra month in the field. He received honors for his work.

Ben took up neurosurgery with great excitement. Soon, several doctors were allowing him to make rounds with them and care for their patients. Ben loved every minute of the work. His dream was coming true. It was not quite the same as his original dream of becoming a missionary doctor. But neurosurgery was just as exciting to him as the stories he had heard as a child in church.

In the fall of 1976, Ben was ready to begin his internship, which is an advanced training program.

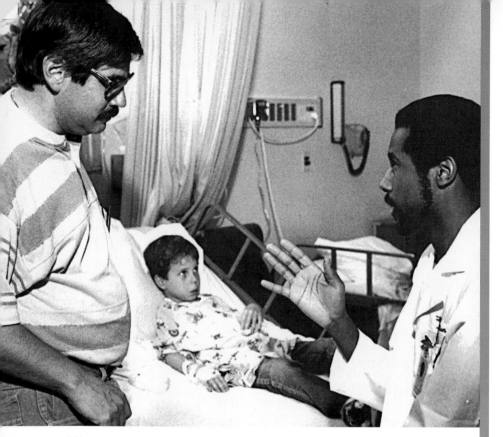

While Ben faced racism on the job, his skill and concern won him the respect of most of his patients and coworkers.

For this, he applied to Johns Hopkins Hospital in Baltimore, Maryland. Johns Hopkins received over 125 applications to join their neurosurgery division each year. They accepted only two. This did not scare Ben Carson. His mother's words echoed in his mind: He could become whatever he wanted to be.

Ben's interview at Johns Hopkins went very well. His interviewer was pleased with Ben's school records. He also noticed Ben's interest in classical music. The interviewer loved classical music. The experience proved to Ben that no knowledge is ever wasted. Johns Hopkins accepted Ben's application, and he transferred there in 1977.

Two years earlier, in 1975, Ben and Candy had married. In Baltimore, they took a small apartment, and Candy found a job. Candy also returned to school and earned a master's degree in business. She went on to work for the Mercantile Bank and Trust. Like Ben, Candy was hardworking and driven to succeed.

As an intern, Ben discovered a great deal about medicine and the way people treat each other. He noticed that some doctors showed little respect for the nurses and other staff. Ben felt differently. As far as he was concerned, the nurses and the aides were professionals, too. They knew a lot about the hospital, and had much to teach him.

Ben also learned to deal with the attitude some people had toward him. In the beginning of his internship, some nurses would ask Ben to pick up a patient or carry out bed linen. They thought that because Ben was African-American, he must be an orderly. They did not stop to think he might be a doctor.

Some patients had the same attitude. When they met Ben for the first time, they asked when the doctor would arrive. Other patients did not let Ben touch them—just because he was black. Even one of the doctors gave Ben a hard time. He seemed to feel that an African-American intern did not belong at Johns

Hopkins. This person was jealous that Ben's good work was drawing a lot of positive attention.

Word got around the hospital about these racist words and feelings. The chairman of the neurosurgery department, Dr. Donlin Long, was quick to let people know they had two choices: accept Ben or find the exit. As far as Ben knows, no one ever walked out.

Ben was grateful to Dr. Long for his support. He did not allow the racism to get to him. His mother had often said, "It doesn't really matter what color you are. If you're good, you will be recognized." Now, her words were proving true.

Ben finished his two-year internship in just one year. In 1978, he was invited to become a resident, or new doctor, in the Johns Hopkins neurosurgery department. Dr. Carson was a resident from 1978 until 1982. He also spent a short time in 1981 as a senior resident at Baltimore City Hospital. It was there that an inexperienced Ben Carson met one of the first great challenges in his work. He was forced to perform a dangerous operation on his own.

It began when a man was rushed through the doors of the Baltimore City emergency room. The patient had been badly beaten with a baseball bat. He was bleeding from the head. Already in a **coma**, the man was unable to respond to doctors. He was dying. No senior surgeon was available to operate on the man. Filled with fear, Ben saw he had to take care of the patient, and fast. He would have to perform the operation himself. Ben quickly set up an operating team. They opened the man's skull. Because his head had been hit, there was a lot of swelling in the man's brain. Ben was able to ease the swelling by taking out parts of the damaged brain. The operation was a success. It was the first of many great successes in the operating room for Ben Carson.

In 1982, Ben did some research that helped other doctors learn more about how brain **tumors** grow. His discovery was an important step in the fight against cancer. It was not Ben's work alone that was amazing. It was also the speed with which he did it. What should have taken years, Dr. Carson managed to

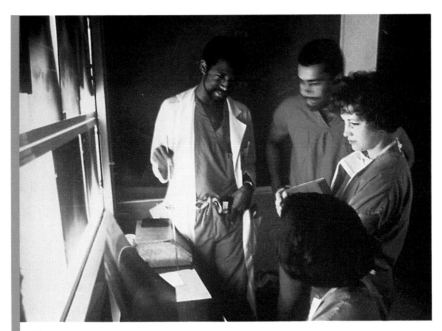

Ben Carson is a firm believer in teamwork. He works with teams of medical professionals both in and out of the operating room.

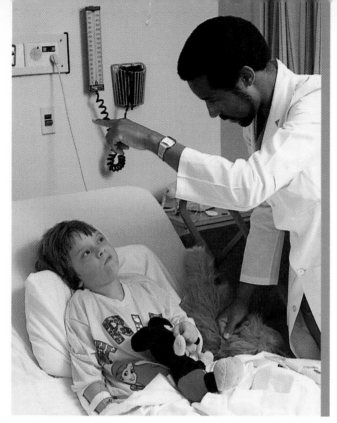

As Chief of Pediatric Neurosurgery at Johns Hopkins, Ben needs a special kind of skill to work with children and their parents.

do in six months. His ability to gather information and work with a team was really paying off. For his hard work, Ben won the Resident-of-the-Year Award.

In June 1983, Ben and Candy Carson made a big move. They decided to go to Perth, Australia. Ben had been invited to practice at the Queen Elizabeth II Medical Center. The salary for his one-year residency was $65,000. In 1983, that was a lot of money for a doctor's first-year position.

Before moving, the Carsons were worried about racism in Australia. Ben and Candy had heard that it was worse than in South Africa. To their surprise, the Carsons were warmly welcomed by the hospital staff when they arrived in Perth. They were also greeted by a congregation of Seventh-Day Adventists. Members of the church made sure that the Carson family had plenty of friends.

During his one-year term in Perth, Ben Carson got a lot of experience in the operating room. Many of his operations were on children. Once again, his skills, dedication, and personality won the respect of many of the staff and patients.

Ben's success in the hospital was not the only reason to celebrate. On September 12, 1983, Candy Carson gave birth to their first son, Murray Nedlands Carson. Not long after that, Ben's year in Australia was finished. The Carsons flew back to Baltimore.

Ben did not have to wait long to see where his future would take him. That same year, the Chief of Pediatric Neurosurgery at Johns Hopkins quit his job. Dr. Donlin Long quickly suggested that Ben Carson take the job. The hospital's board of directors agreed. At 33, Ben became the youngest Chief of Pediatric Neurosurgery in United States history.

Now, really important cases began to come Ben's way. In 1985, Ben met the four-year-old Maranda Francisco. For three years, Maranda's parents had been taking her to doctors. No one had been able to figure out how to help her. Now, in one last act of hope, they brought her to Ben Carson at Johns Hopkins.

Maranda had a form of **epilepsy** called grand mal seizures. This meant that her body would go into violent fits. Sometimes she was unable to move her right side. Maranda was having as many as a hundred seizures each day.

It was up to Ben to see if he could save the girl. He got help from Dr. Neville Knuckey, a surgeon he had met in Australia. Together they prepared for a dangerous operation called a hemispherectomy. In this operation, they would take out a part of the left side of the brain. If the doctors did it right, Maranda would be free of her seizures. If they failed, she could die.

The night before the operation, Dr. Carson went over all the details of the operation with Maranda's parents. At the end of this long talk, Ben gave the Franciscos some homework to do. It was the same homework he gave every child's parents before an operation. He asked them to pray.

The next morning came, and the operation began. After ten hours of surgery, Maranda had lost huge amounts of blood. But she had gained so much more. When Maranda woke up and opened her eyes, her first words were, "I love you, Mommy and Daddy." The surgery had worked!

The operation was big news. Newspapers and TV talk shows wanted to interview the surgeon and the child. Ben shied away from most of the spotlight. As far as he was concerned, he had simply done his job. Still, the eyes of the medical world and the media were watching Dr. Ben Carson. They wanted to see what he would do next.

By the mid-1980s, Ben Carson's amazing success with very difficult operations had come to the attention of the media and the public.

Ben was soon thrown back into the spotlight. Theresa and Josef Binder needed his help. The Binders had come to Johns Hopkins University all the way from Germany. They had seven-month-old **Siamese twins** who needed to be separated.

Benjamin and Patrick Binder had been born joined at the back of the head. The twins had different personalities and sleeping habits. They were definitely two separate people, but as long as they were joined like this, they would never be able to walk, play, or even rise from bed on their own.

Ben Carson was thrilled by the chance to help the children. He was excited about the challenges of the operation. He was also worried. There had never been a successful separation of twins joined at the head. It was a huge and dangerous task.

Ben got to work. The surgical team that would operate on the boys was made up of over seventy people. Dr. Carson and Dr. Long were involved in months of planning. Ben even flew to Germany to see the boys before they came to the United States. Five months of preparation passed. On September 5, 1987, at 7:15 A.M., the twin boys went into surgery. The operation was even more complicated than Ben had expected it to be. The clock ticked away. Every second counted for Dr. Carson and his team. Once they separated the twins, they stopped the boys' hearts and their blood flow. This gave the surgeons time to construct separate veins for each boy's head. If they took any longer than an hour, the boys would suffer very bad brain damage. The doctors made it with only seconds to spare.

Then, when their hearts started pumping again, both boys began losing huge amounts of blood. The blood supply in the hospital ran out. People in the operating room quickly offered to give their own blood, but they did not have to. The American Red Cross was able to supply the blood.

Then the brains of both children began to swell. If the team did not move fast enough, the brains would

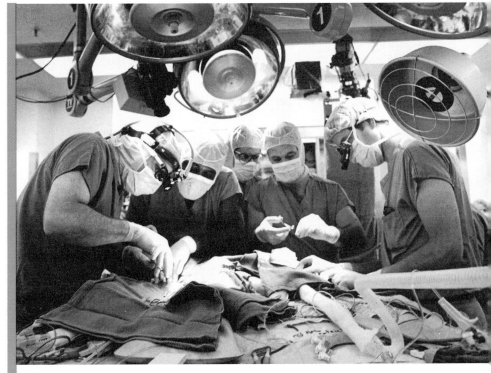

To separate Siamese twins joined at the back of the head, Dr. Carson and his team spent 22 hours in the OR.

begin to come right out of the openings in the boys' skulls! Dr. Carson and Dr. Long quickly finished their work and closed up the skulls.

The operation ended on September 6, at 5:15 P.M. Twenty-two hours earlier, Benjamin and Patrick Binder had entered the operating room together. Now they exited the room on two separate tables.

The boys were kept in a coma for ten days to allow their brains to recover. For those ten long days, Dr. Carson had no idea how well the twins would survive—or if they would survive at all. There was still the chance of something very bad happening.

Cries of joy filled the halls of Johns Hopkins when the boys opened their eyes and began to move. The babies had made it! They now had a chance to lead normal lives. Once again, Dr. Ben Carson had done the impossible.

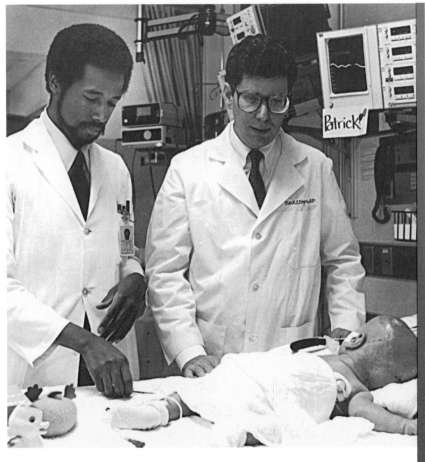

Ben Carson and another member of the surgical team examine Patrick Binder, one of the twins, after surgery.

Chapter Six

"DON'T BELIEVE THE HYPE"

Ben Carson has come a long way since the days of being a frightened eight-year-old child. He has crossed color lines in his work. He has struggled against racial prejudice. His skills and intelligence have won him many great rewards.

With patience and faith, Ben has overcome every hurdle on his way to his dream. He did not live the life that too many people expect a black youth from the ghetto to live. By pushing himself, he has become not only a great doctor, but also a respected one. Word of Ben Carson's inspiring success has reached thousands of people. In 1990, Ben even wrote his autobiography, or life story, called *Gifted Hands.*

Professional success is not Ben Carson's only source of happiness. In his struggle to find peace with himself, Ben has stayed true to his religious faith. No success has touched his life without his giving thanks in prayer.

Although his skills are very much in demand, Ben Carson always makes time for his family. Here Ben relaxes in his front yard with his wife Candy and their three sons, Murray, Ben, Jr., and Rhoeyce.

His greatest joy and success, Ben believes, is his family. On May 26, 1985, Ben and Candy Carson welcomed their second child, Benjamin Carson, Jr., into the world. On December 21, 1986, their third son, Rhoeyce Carson, was born.

With a wife and three sons, Ben decided that sharing time with his family should always come first. Perhaps Ben remembered how hard it had been when his own father left him. He wanted to do things very differently. Ben Carson knows that his wife and his children will always be able to depend on him.

Ben Carson has never forgotten the love and encouragement he got from his mother. Her work and words certainly paid off. Ben became a gifted neurosurgeon. His brother Curtis served in the navy, graduated from college, and became a successful engineer. The Carson family has been a success, through and through!

Children are very important to Ben. Each day he works to save and improve their lives. He also speaks at schools and community centers to tell children how he reached his goals in life. He tries to give them hope and a feeling of power.

Dr. Carson tells young people not to listen to the negative things they hear about their race, religion, or how much money their families have. He encourages them to work hard and believe in themselves.

Ben warns children, especially African-American children, not to allow others to decide how far they can go in life. There was a time in Ben's life when that kind of negative thinking led him nowhere but down. Today he is living proof you do not have to walk the road of rage and violence.

"Don't believe the hype," Ben urges his young audiences. "Believe in you." With a role model like Dr. Benjamin Carson, who would not want to try?

Important Dates

1951   Born in Detroit, Michigan.

1959   Father leaves, and family moves to Boston.

1961   Family returns to Detroit.

1967   Enters South Western High School. Joins ROTC program.

1969   Wins scholarship to Yale University to study medicine.

1973   Graduates from Yale and enters the University of Michigan Medical School.

1975   Marries Lacena Candy Rustin.

1977   Accepted to internship program at Johns Hopkins Hospital.

1978   Begins residency in neurosurgery department.

1981   Performs first unsupervised brain surgery.

1982   Develops new method of researching and scanning brain tumors. Completes residency at Johns Hopkins.

1983   Works in Perth, Australia.

1984   Returns to the U.S. and becomes the Chief of Pediatric Neurosurgery at Johns Hopkins.

1985   Performs his first hemispherectomy.

1987   Performs the first successful separation of Siamese twins joined at the back of the head.

1990   First publication of his autobiography, *Gifted Hands*.

Glossary

coma A state of unconsciousness, like a deep sleep, usually from a brain injury.

epilepsy A brain disease which causes sudden unconsciousness and/or violent fits.

neurosurgery An operation performed on the brain or the central nervous system.

pediatrics The area of medicine concerned with the care and treatment of children's diseases.

scalpel A surgical knife.

Siamese twins Twins born with their bodies or heads connected.

tumors Diseased growths found in the body.

Bibliography

Bleich, Alan R. *Exploring Careers in Medicine*. New York: Rosen, 1990.

Carson, Ben, with Cecil Murphey and Nathan Aaseng. *Ben Carson* (Today's Heroes Series). Grand Rapids, MI: Zondervan, 1993.

Carson, Ben, with Cecil Murphey. *Gifted Hands*. Grand Rapids, MI: Zondervan, 1990.